Watch This!

A book about making shapes

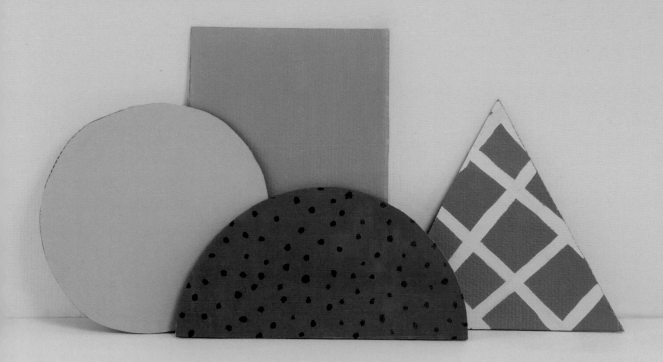

Watch This!

A book about making shapes

Izzy

Leo

Jasmine

Jane Godwin, Beci Orpin
& Hilary Walker

SCRIBBLE

For Trixie Maher – Jane

For Zedrin and Tahlin – Beci

For Ben and Sonny – Hilary

Thank you to Gabriel Cole, Zoe Harriet,
Chris Middlebrooke, Ai Nishimoto, Joseph Saad
for your work on the sets.

The background sets were made using large cardboard sheets,
cut-paper and paint.

Published by Scribble, an imprint of Scribe Publications, 2018
18–20 Edward Street, Brunswick, Victoria 3056, Australia
2 John Street, Clerkenwell, London, WC1N 2ES, United Kingdom

Text © Jane Godwin 2018
Art Direction © Beci Orpin 2018
Photography © Hilary Walker 2018

Printed and bound in China by Leo Paper Products Ltd

9781925322774 (Australian hardback)
9781911344957 (UK hardback)

CiP records for this title are available from the
National Library of Australia and the British Library

scribblekidsbooks.com
scribepublications.com.au

Luisa can make a circle with her arms.

Izzy can make a triangle
if she keeps her body straight,

or we can make a triangle like this.

Jasmine can make a little triangle with her fingers,

or a big square
with a friend.

If we sit with straight legs out, what shape do we make?

Edie can make a semi-circle with only her self.

Now let's make a big circle.
Edie...Marlo...Saskia...Ari.
No corners, just curves.

But look,
Ari and Luisa have
made a new shape!
A diamond.

What about a rectangle? It needs four corners.

Here's a rectangle with a roof. It looks like a house!

Saskia can jump on her footprints,

and Izzy can walk on her hands – if Leo helps.

We
can
make
a
straight
line,

a wavy line,

and a zig-zag, if we all bend in half.

You can do it, Iris!

Let's try a pyramid.
Watch this...
One, two, three...

It's a bit wobbly.
Hold on, Niko!

Now we need a rest.

I know, let's make up some new shapes of our own.

Watch this! We've made a table out of us.

This shape has six arms. It's an Ari-tangle!

Let's hold hands like this.
Now we're all joined together,

what shapes do you see?

That was fun,
and the very
last one…

Saskia, your tummy's rumbling!

What shapes can you make?